The Lonely Snowman

Written by ANGELA HOLROYD

Illustrated by ROWAN CLIFFORD

Derrydale Books

New York/Avenel, New Jersey

A TEMPLAR BOOK

This 1992 edition published by Derrydale Books,
distributed by Outlet Book Company, Inc., a Random House Company,
40 Engelhard Avenue, Avenel, New Jersey 07001.

First published in Canada in 1992 by Smithbooks,
113 Merton Street, Toronto, Canada M45 1AB.

Devised and produced by The Templar Company plc,
Pippbrook Mill, London Road, Dorking, Surrey RH4 1JE, Great Britain.

Copyright © 1992 by The Templar Company plc
Illustrations copyright © 1992 by The Templar Company plc

Edited by Wendy Madgwick
Designed by Janie Louise Hunt
Printed and bound in Singapore

ISBN 0-517-06969-5
8 7 6 5 4 3 2 1

When Charlie's mother had to go into the hospital, his father sent him to his grandparents to be looked after. His grandma baked delicious cookies and his grandpa told wonderful stories. They even allowed Charlie to take his dog, Pip, with him but Charlie still felt lonely.

He missed his parents and he missed his friends. His grandparents lived miles away from anywhere and Charlie had no one to play with.

One night, snow fell. Charlie woke in the morning and looked out of his bedroom window. It looked as if the whole world had been painted white. Feeling excited, Charlie raced downstairs for breakfast and then pulled on his warmest clothes and best rubber boots. Whistling for Pip, he dashed out of the door.

But once he was out in the snow-covered yard, he suddenly remembered that there were no other children to play with.

Back home, he and his friends would have had glorious snowball fights, made slippery slides, and built snowmen with bright coal eyes and carrot noses. They would have played outside until Charlie's mom called them in for cups of soup and hot buttered toast. But no one was waiting for him today — he and Pip were all alone.

Charlie looked over the yard gate and across the fields to the dark woods in the distance. There was not a single living thing to be seen anywhere. It was as if he and Pip were the only ones awake, ready to play and have fun in the dazzling snowy landscape.

"Ah well, Pip," sighed Charlie, looking at the snow-white hill that rose up behind the yard. "It's just you and me I suppose. Come on, I'll race you to those woods!"

So the pair chased each other up the hill until they reached the woods at the top. Charlie flung himself down on the soft, snowy ground and tried to get his breath back. Pip ran off into the woods to explore. But he soon came bounding back, barking loudly.

"What is it boy?" asked Charlie. "What have you found?"

Pip tugged at Charlie's sleeve and pulled him deeper into the woods. When Charlie saw what had frightened Pip, he could hardly believe his eyes. There in the middle of the pathway stood a snowman with the saddest face Charlie had ever seen. Pip flattened himself on the ground and whined.

"It's alright, Pip," Charlie said comfortingly. "It's only a snowman, but I wonder who built him and why he looks so sad?" The snowman really did look very miserable and lonely.

"I think he's even more lonely than I am," thought Charlie. "At least I have Pip and grandma and grandpa."

Then Charlie had a great idea. Quickly he started to scoop up the snow.

"Don't you worry anymore, Mr. Snowman," he whispered. "I'm going to build you a family to keep you company."

Charlie worked hard all morning. First, he made the snowman a wife. He used small stones for her eyes and a row of bright red berries to give her a cheery smile.

Charlie grinned in delight, then set about gathering up masses more snow. Taking great care, he made two smaller snowchildren with red berry smiles.

He stepped back and looked at the snow family. He fancied that the snowman had started to smile. Charlie, feeling really pleased with all his hard work, called for Pip to come and see.

Pip, who had been off exploring again, came running to his side. He took one look at the snow figures and began pawing at Charlie's hand. Then he padded over to the snowchildren and sat next to them.

Charlie burst out laughing — it was the first time he had laughed for days.

"So you think that they should have a dog too, do you, Pip?"

It took Charlie quite a long time to make a snow dog, and when he had finished he realized that he was late for lunch.

"I've got to go now," he told the snow family. "But I'll be back tomorrow."

Charlie's grandmother had been worried about him — it wasn't like Charlie to be late for meals. But she didn't scold him, once he had explained about the snowman and how he had built him a snow family.

"Come on and eat," she said. "And then we'll go up into the attic and find some old hats and scarves for your snow family."

"Oh, great!" said Charlie, giving his grandma a hug.

He ate his lunch as quickly as he could, then followed his grandparents up the narrow stairs to the top of the house. The attic was like an Aladdin's cave — tin boxes and chests, old carpets and pictures, lamps

and shades littered the floors and walls. There were even some old wooden skis from grandpa's schooldays!

Charlie spent a very happy hour trying on hats and scarves. His grandpa even found him a cute collar for the snow dog.

Next morning, Charlie woke up early. His grandma encouraged him to eat a good, hot breakfast, then he and Pip headed back to the woods. His grandparents watched and smiled. It was good to see their grandson happy again.

The hats and scarves looked terrific on his
snow family, but the collar on the dog pleased him
the most — it made the dog look almost real! Pip
thought so too. He barked and ran around it as if
inviting the snow dog to play.

Before Charlie went home, he sat on a tree
trunk and told the snow family all about himself.

He explained that his father was in the Navy and away sailing the high seas. His mother was in the hospital, and he missed her and all his friends very much.

"But I won't miss them quite as much now," he said. "Because I have all of you. I will come and visit you every day."

And that is exactly what Charlie did. Every day he went to the woods to see his snow family and that is why he noticed something very strange — every day they seemed to be in a different position!

Then one day Charlie woke up very early to a strange sound. DRIP! DRIP! DRIP! it went. The snow was melting on the roof and dripping outside his bedroom window. It had begun to thaw!

"My snow family!" Charlie cried out in horror. "If the snow is melting, they'll melt too!"

Without even stopping long enough to tell his grandparents where he was going, Charlie and Pip rushed off to the woods. They found the snow family standing outside a tumbledown shack. Charlie rushed up to the snowman and flung his arms around him, tears streaming down his face.

"It's starting to thaw," he sobbed. "And you will all melt and I don't know how to stop it!"

To his surprise, he felt a cold arm go around his shoulders.

"It's alright Charlie, don't cry," said a kindly voice. "We're going to the North Pole where there's snow all year round. We'll be safe there."

Charlie stepped back and blinked hard. The snowman was looking down at him. His wife and the snowchildren came forward smiling their red-berry smiles. They danced round Charlie, chuckling with glee. The snowdog rubbed noses with Pip and they began playing tag.

Charlie was astounded.

"You can ... can walk, and ... and talk!" he stammered.

"Of course," answered the snowman. "Nearly all snowfolk can."

"But why haven't you spoken before?" asked Charlie, still unable to believe his ears.

"We are supposed to keep it a secret," said one of the snowchildren.

"But you have shown us so much kindness and love that we couldn't go away without thanking you," said the other, putting his arm around Charlie.

"Yes," said the snowman. "I had to stay to thank you for making me such a lovely family to keep me company."

Charlie sat down heavily and rubbed his eyes. Surely he must be dreaming. But, no! When he looked up, there they were as large as life, smiling down at him. He grinned back.

"I shall miss you," he said. "But at least I know you'll be safe and happy at the North Pole."

The two snowchildren pulled Charlie to his feet, dancing around in their excitement. The snowman and his wife joined in the merry jig and the two dogs pranced along behind.

On and on they trudged, deeper and deeper into the heart of the woods. Charlie noticed that there were places where the snow had almost melted completely. He was sad that his snow family had to go away, but he was glad to know that they would be safe. There would be no danger of them melting at the North Pole — it was always freezing cold there. The little group hurried on, following Fern through the dark woods.

Farther and farther they traveled. Charlie could see that the sun was already beginning to set and, what's more, his snow family were beginning to look softer and thinner. He was so worried and afraid for his friends. He closed his eyes and wished with all his might that they would reach the Polar Express before the snow people melted away forever. Just then Fern stopped and turned to them.

"This is where I must leave you," she said. She pointed her nose down a track where two large rabbits were waiting. "They will take you the rest of the way."

"How much farther is it?" Charlie asked Fern anxiously.

"Not far now," she reassured him. "You will be there before nightfall." And with that she disappeared.

The travelers followed the fluffy white tails of the rabbits and discovered that Fern had been right. Just as the moon began to show her face, the rabbits stopped in a small clearing.

"This is the place," said one of them.

"The Polar Express is due anytime now," added the other and, with a flash of their tails, they too disappeared into the undergrowth.

Suddenly Charlie heard a faint whistle. It was the train! The whistle grew louder and louder as the train came closer but Charlie could see no sign of it in the gloom of the forest. The snowchildren jumped up and down with excitement as, to Charlie's amazement, the train appeared, flying through the sky above them. It descended into the clearing with a great SWOOSH!

A great white train that Charlie was amazed to find
was made entirely of snow. Everyone cheered. The
train driver, a smiling snowman wearing a blue cap,
waved to them. The guard at the back climbed down.
   "All aboard for the North Pole," he cried
loudly. It was time for the snow family to leave.

Charlie hugged each of them in turn and patted the snow dog's head. Once they were safely in their seats, the guard climbed back on to the train and blew his whistle.

"Goodbye! Goodbye!" called the snowman. "I will always remember you, Charlie. For without you I would have remained lonely all my life. Thank you for making me a family, kind friend. You will not be lonely without us for long. Thank you again, and goodbye!" The train hovered a few inches above the ground, then WHOOSH! It disappeared among the glittering stars.

"Good luck! Good luck all of you!" Charlie called out into the night, but the train and the snow people had gone. Then he looked at Pip sitting patiently at his side.

"It's just you and me again, now," he said sadly. "And we've somehow got to find our way home. It's a long way, Pip, and I'm so tired."

Charlie looked around him. Everywhere looked the same. He wasn't too sure which route would lead him back home. He yawned and slumped down.

"Perhaps I'll just have a little rest before we start back ...." Yawning again, he put his arm around Pip and within the blink of an eye fell fast asleep.

As he slept the animals of the forest crept out to keep watch over him, making sure that he came to no harm. The stillness of night closed in around him and from far away came the magical sound of the Polar Express as it sped on its way to the North Pole. Charlie stirred in his sleep, but did not wake.

The next thing Charlie knew, he was in his own bed. His grandmother was shaking him awake.

"The hospital has just phoned," she said. "You have a baby brother now Charlie, and your father is coming home soon. He's asked us to take you back this afternoon." Charlie leapt out of bed and hugged his grandma happily. A baby brother!

Then he heard DRIP! DRIP! DRIP! outside the window and remembered his dream. It had only been a dream after all, and now his snow family really would be melting.

Charlie shook his head sadly. His dream had seemed so real.

"I must see them once more before I go,"
Charlie thought to himself.

So he and Pip raced off to the woods for the
last time as soon as breakfast was over, but the snow
family were nowhere to be seen. They searched
everywhere, but there was no sign of them. Charlie
couldn't believe it — how could they have disappeared
so quickly?

"They can't have melted away already," Charlie
told himself. "Anyway, where are their hats and scarves?
And where's the dog's collar? They wouldn't have
melted too."

He shook his head sadly and called to Pip.
They were just about to give up and leave the woods
when Charlie heard a faint, high-pitched whistle. It
sounded just like the whistle of the Polar Express
coming from far, far away.

Charlie looked up into the sky and smiled to himself. No one would ever believe him, but he knew that his snow family were safe and that, like him, his snowman would never be lonely again.